#7
FALL 2025

MIDSUMMER DREAM HOUSE LITERARY & ARTS MAGAZINE

CALIFORNIA

Midsummer Dream House
San Diego, California
United States

Cover Art
by Edward Michael Supranowicz

Paperback ISBN: 979-8-9917450-9-3
Print ISSN: 3064-7819
Printed in the United States

midsummer dream house

Editor-in-Chief
Emma Grey Rose

Editor
George du Bois

CONTENTS

ANDREW BUCKNER

DON'T WORRY TOO MUCH ABOUT PEOPLE (A MESSAGE TO MY DAUGHTERS)

Don't worry too much about people.

They change their minds with the trends.

They will use you and abuse you
And wonder why you don't call them a "friend."

Don't worry too much about people.

They will say they need you, plead to you
And pass you up when the goal post bends.

Don't worry too much about people.

They just want to hurt you, insert in you
A lifetime of insecurity, doubt.

They just want to shout, to blame

You, you, always you!

Don't worry too much about people.

They ask what you can do for them
And never the other way around.

Don't worry too much about people.

Silence is better without all the sound.

TOM SNARSKY

FOREST INTERIOR

The bats fade out into the distance between apostasy and heresy. One blue lung carries the salve in its sound. Yesterday you wounded me mid-picture, the thought of laughter in my painèd
face. I painted you a moon presiding over a harbor. I was proud.

I heard you say *I'm leaving* in the voice of a window. One single headache had become the whole night. I said look and you did, like an embryo in tempera. Like a pumpkin crushed unsuspecting between hippo jaws.

Cruelty can continue. It can be bistre and it can be red. It can be gray. Violins like kittens, mewling, no memory. The substitute for sun waits to be invented. It can be black.

Cruelty can continue. One way to prepare a drawing is to create an array of shapes then ally some—just some—with lines and clouds.

I am waiting for the letters to spill out of your mouth, to search for the lung among them.

Over the harbor hung a tracery of stars.

BERNARD PEARSON

NIGHT TRAIN

So many tunnels
For the red eye
Of grief to go through
Sometimes the dark
Is all consuming
A night of no moon
Where every star
Has crawled away
To the end of the universe
And died and then
There is a glint upon
The window as it
Hurtles who knows where
Its as if those who
 have gone before
have made sure the track
is clear

ALEX RUSSELL

SLAP HAPPY IN PENNSYLVANIA GAS STATIONS

You wouldn't like to stick around to see the end
That's a false line, but I wish I was kinder
There are cries for help I must've misunderstood
I remember drowning in basements, not even
in dreams; it's been at least five years since
I saw you alive; a nightmare, they come & go

Soft steps....flashlights waving themselves
over dark rooftops & tall, slender, old bridges

We haven't talked in days....I wanted to crash
my car into the side of your father's house
I should have come to the funeral

STITCHES/IN MY DREAM LAST NIGHT

Lucy's husband stopped loving me; disgust
and confusion. The 1975 broke up in my dream
last night; it was post-ironic: disgust and
confusion. Even the sunrise was tired this
morning; the world groaned a little, weathering
out the night w/ me only.

ODE TO SAINTS OF PARK BENCH POETS

i think i would like to be drunk with you, tangle-foot wrapped in holiday cheer, and split a cigarette on the rooftop. my daydreams stumble in and out lackadaisical conjuring mango-matcha smoothies, grinning wide, and tongue to the roof of my mouth. you are saint of park bench poet, crown chakra botanist, i'd wander the curl around your lips freestanding sighteyed. our fingers crisscrossed applesauce, cat eye makeup piercing skindrum, i wish i knew your temperament a little better. fair me well, shout streetpreacher a tiny bit wild like i would chew up anything non congruent with jasmine upon request. dmt is a temple of eyelids where my moment to moment resides and maybe we can share another cigarette after dinner. i'm just as lonely.

GABRIEL IS LEFT IN 20-SOMETHING PURGATORY

Penelope spirited through old furniture fires on 10th street eulogies; the last chords of summer mixtapes unfurled and degraded to the point of abstraction.

Gabriel thought it was somewhere around one in the morning the 4-track rattled his sinuses and he was caught gasoline-breath for his neighbors pounding on the wall.

I'd like to leave these two here, all junkie heavens with tattered notebooks, guitars strewn about a racket for
recording halls teeth numb and rambling.

This, a narrative of early twenties gathered in substance effigies, a handful of unfinished songs and albums,
directionless. Someone pick up the check.

I guess what I mean to say is: we pulled the light bulbs for pockets and mouthful, a grin so wide we were lockjaw. I'm done romanticizing our vagrancy.

I'll be honest, I miss them, but their penniless crescendos for rafters isn't cognizance. Its hands are spectral metaphysics wrapped tightly 'round ventricles.

MILENA FILIPPS

WHEN SUNLIGHT MEETS A TREE

Every evening, a ray of sunlight descends to a forgotten garden and leans on a tree. This tree is young and thin compared to its peers standing a bit further away, still wearing their heavy coats of dark leaves at the end of summer. All those leaves, much larger than my hands, sing an old hymn that is instantly picked up by wind and carried away to places much different from a green idyll.

When sunlight meets a tree, it falls on a trunk that has not witnessed a whole century yet, but it has heard the wind speak almost every day for the last few decades. A ray of sunlight never brings a song to sing, a ballad to recite, a melody to whisper – and so the leaves of every tree, pale and dark, green, brown and yellow, remain indifferent to its presence, as much as they do not care about their own shadow. They barely notice this grey phantom stretched on the ground beneath them, sometimes imitating the shape of two specific branches, just like a ghost may imitate the voice once attributed to the name on the ghost's gravestone. Sunlight experiments with this shape, as the wind forms the language of trees. The grey spot on the ground may be as transparent as a fallen cloud, or marked by edges as sharp as if they were drawn by an architect's pencil. A quiet companion as familiar as the restless air.

Our own thoughts envy the variety and beauty of the evening's colour and the fleeting contrasts sunlight paints in the garden. We interpret them as a synthesis of change and eternity, two strange concepts we admire for providing a clear dichotomy, ready to be projected on all particularities of life, such as a broken watch, a dying flower or an abandoned garden. Becoming accessible and yet mysterious when reflected by art.

Sunlight only ever leaves the tree to rest at night. It is there to make its drawings in the earliest morning hours, but for some reason we choose to believe the evening to be the time of a long-awaited meeting, most probably because of a random impression we once stumbled upon at that hour and then put on a pedestal. Yet beauty is not the only paradigm capable of guiding our perceptions. There may be another reason why we are so drawn to that visible collision of time and time, growth and passing, roots once laid in the earth by a gardener and a ghostly substance without any clear shape. As we watch the sunlight lay on a tree's shoulder, we cannot see beyond our sad, boring, conventional, static dreams, yet we sense the imperfections of our own mind and the art it produces. Thus, we cling to a question, the need for a final decision. What is this place to our thoughts - a garden or a graveyard?

First published by *Livina Press* (2023)

Issue 6, p. 87

KAFKAESQUE

In Prague, tourists are drawn to an astronomical clock which dates from 1410. I shot a video of it through the rain when I was there. Besides telling time, the *Orloj* (clock) shows astronomical signs, old Czech time, phases of the moon, and a parade of Jesus's Apostles. The clock face itself is framed by figures representing Vanity, Greed, Death, and Lust. Watching my rain-soaked video, I try to make sense of all of these working parts, but I've never quite mastered it all. Franz Kafka would have walked past this clock in the Old Town Square on the daily, and I wonder if he recognized and understood all of the aspects of the clock. Did he, like me, find it overwhelming and confusing? Would it be correct to call it...Kafkaesque? I've always associated the words nightmarish, complex, surreal, phantasmagorical, and bizarre to define the word Kafkaesque. These words also apply to an experience I had in a college discussion of Franz Kafka's "The Metamorphosis" thirty-eight years ago which still haunts me.

If you haven't read the story, it centers around Gregor Samsa, a traveling salesman who wakes up one day transformed into an insect (cockroach or dung beetle depending on the translation) with numerous uncontrollable little legs. He has to deal with his new situation as well as his family's reactions. The other humans in his life did not understand his screechy speech, but to Gregor it sounded normal. Of course, there are many intellectual/academic interpretations of this story. Since the author is Franz Kafka, and I've studied some Kafka, I believe the central theme is that Gregor Samsa wished to withdraw from his human responsibilities, mostly helping to support his family. I always thought it was touching that he paid for his sister, Grete's, violin lessons at the Conservatorium. After his metamorphosis, her violin lessons go away and his parents' situation becomes lean.

Gregor's contribution to his sister's musical interests was a good investment, because as it turned out, she would be the one to feed and take care of him after his transmutation. This ended when Grete and their parents were forced to return to work. They were too busy to pay much attention to him and he became lonely. Other humans, uncomfortable with Gregor's transformation, avoided him. This human reaction is taken straight out of reality: how many times have we seen or experienced people not knowing what to say or do in response to a death, divorce, or crisis, and then they say or do nothing? I have, and it makes the hurt hurt more.

Gregor ultimately dies, and no one but the charwoman will tend to his body. The reader is left to wonder what might have happened to his corpse, but Kafka extends the nightmare by placing a butcher's assistant in the building. It seems that his place of employment specializes in sausages.

I wrote about the twentieth century classroom experience before, in a travel essay about Prague in which I explored Kafka's legacy there. As I think about this short story, the surreal classroom experience bubbles up again. Not three years before that class, during my senior year of high school, my father suffered a massive stroke which turned everything upside-down for my family.

In college, I kept my focus on school, and signed up for that summer Short Story course to earn some required English credits. We read and discussed anthologies full of short stories and I grew an appreciation for the genre. It was an intellectually inspiring six weeks, except for the day we sat down to discuss "The Metamorphosis."

I explained how after my father had a stroke, people were different towards him. In a nutshell, in that class I compared the reactions of people around Gregor Samsa as cockroach to reactions of people around my father post-stroke. My father's best work friend, a church deacon, would visit often and engage Dad in one-sided conversations which Dad appreciated. Visits from family dropped off, though, except for my sister and her family, occasionally. I could see it most clearly in the reactions of her three elementary-school-aged kids: this man looked like Grandpa, but everything was different about him. Not knowing what to do, they retreated and avoided interacting with him at all. I don't blame them—they were kids. I wasn't navigating this situation well myself. Gregor Samsa's transformation into a bug alienated his family, and with my father it was his new inability to walk, talk, feed himself, or change television channels. I imagined that my father felt like Gregor the bug on the inside, and like Gregor he could not express feelings.

I thought my connection between Gregor Samsa and my father was profound and personal. It was unlike anything I had ever shared in a classroom situation before. I looked at the students' faces. A few looked back at me, but most were studying their notes or their shoes. They were retreating from the discussion. I looked over at the professor expecting some kind of reaction or at least a thank-you-for-sharing. I got nothing.

I felt like a cockroach now.

I finished the course because I needed those three credits. I never offered anything in that classroom again, not to punish them, but to save myself from having to relive anything like that Kafkaesque experience. My father's stroke and its aftermath taught me to always do something for people suffering loss or crisis, even if it's a simple note. My "Metamorphosis" experience taught me to consider even the most preposterous interpretation of literature or life as valid.

As a reference librarian in a college, I help students research literary criticism to support their ideas in the required ten-page research paper. They rarely select "The Metamorphosis" for this task. Once, though, a student brainstormed out loud to me about Gregor Samsa's story: "I just don't understand what it *means*!"

"Well," I said, sensing I was about to step into a Kafkaesque phantasmagoria, "I can tell you what it means to me." She invited me to continue, so I gave her a nutshell version of my 38-year-old college comments. Rather than studying her shoes, she watched me, nodding and understanding. When I finished, she exclaimed, "OH! I get it now!" That statement validated the Kafkaesque classroom situation that has burdened me for 38 years. It was a long wait.

Recently, I read the story again to make sure my facts and references here checked out. It occurred to me upon that recent reading that Gregor was not the only Samsa to go through a metamorphosis. Grete and her parents are described as benefitting from their new working lives necessitated by Gregor's inability to work. Once he was gone, they seemed optimistic. They looked to the future and thought about finding a husband for Grete. They were blooming, or is it blossoming, but Gregor Samsa's life seemed even more tragic.

THE BOOK OF AWEN

In loving dedication to Indiana Ryder Cooley, the Red Eagle, & Nina "Bonita" Bresloff

PART I

The Void & the Mind

Before the sea, sky or land, there was only the Void - an infinite emptiness, dark and still. Yet within the silence stirred a thought, nameless and formless. For endless eons it gradually gained awareness, until it realized itself as Mind.

Filled with curiosity, Mind imagined - and a song of creation burst forth into being. First came a sea of chaotic energies, swirling and sparking like an ocean of tumultuous storm. Next Mind sang a song of the sky, bringing stabilizing forces to temper the raw magic of the waters below.

Delighted, Mind danced between sea and sky, weaving patterns from their synergy. Wherever its presence passed, the fabrics of existence grew firm and vibrant. Then Mind had a new inspiration - to create a gateway between realms.

As Mind danced and sang, strands of sea and sky trailed its movements, weaving as they flowed. A matrix formed - filigrees wrapping the void, threads rooting below and shooting above at intervals. These glistening lattices thickened into conduits linking the embryonic earth to watery abyss and celestial ethers.

Gradually the woven strands amassed - no longer a veil but a colossal tree embracing all creation. Its tangled root system delved through the domain of consorting sea gods, while soaring boughs crested the heavens where sky deities vied and mated.

There stood the first Oak tree, mighty Beh, binding earth to sky and sea. And along its mammoth trunk and limbs, the roads between realms were formed as channels linking the ever growing material and spiritual worlds. Mind settled in Beh's boughs, watching its awakened dreams slowly come to life. The great tree's slumbering acorn children would soon sprout to populate all corners of existence.

And Mind knew this was but the dawning, with endless new wonders to imagine into the weaving cosmic tapestry.

The Seeds of Life

As Mind slipped into peaceful slumber within the boughs of mighty Beh, the great tree continued its silent work of steadying form from the void's potential. Its plunging roots funneling the creative flux of the underworld upward through root and branch. The leaves of its far-spread crown sifting celestial streams of sky-fire pulled from the protective breath of Beh, channeling their illumination into new shapes and patterns.

Where these ascending and descending tides converged within the veins of Beh's wood, a sap of primordial elements brewed brimming with generative power. Two vessels took shape beneath the waving leaves. Acorns were they. And they swelled until they shimmered with holy luster. One blazed as an almost blinding ruby, while the other flickered moon-like- as if pearl.

When the acorns' glossy hulls could no longer contain the indwelling force gathered from Beh's sap, they burst asunder. Unfurling from their shattered cases emerged radiant godlings. The Dagda, muscular and ruddy...and his shining sister Brigid, luminous as quicksilver. Beh had crafted mighty vessels to steward the flowering earth.

As Dagda and Brigid gained their footing upon the burgeoning world, Mind awakened once more. "Go now my children into the domains of sea, land and sky," It spoke. "Master their mysteries, set their chaotic voices to a noble symphony, and summon new life through the authority granted you by sacred Beh, binder of all realms."

The two looked upon one another and the barren landscape before them and each smiled to the other, awaiting the euphoria of genesis.

The Lovers

Dagda and Brigid raced across the nascent earth, splashing through shining waters and rolling hills. Soaring upon the winds. Willing creation into fantastical expression. Every tryst saw new mixtures of form take shape - fins morphed to limbs, scales to fur, tendrils to feathered wings. Soon a bounty of birds, beasts and flowering plants gloried the realms.

Yet unknown to the frolicking pair, far more ancient powers were stirring in ethereal dimensions beyond earthly sight. For as Dagda and Brigid fanned the flames of life through matter's kingdoms, within the luminous celestial spheres churned Woden - lord of wisdom, law and searing illumination. And in the dark oceanic abyss of the underworld formed Ceridwen - the ageless crone, weaving the blood flow of destiny with her shadowed threads.

At times, Woden and Ceridwen turned their gaze upon creation's flowering, blessing favorable developments and cursing those overstepping sacred bounds. And on rare occasions, these transcendent forces would become smitten with the mixed beings born of earth, sea or sky - joining in strange union to birth wondrous or terrible entities possessing traits of all planes.

But the goddess and god took little direct part in unfolding reality, choosing instead to channel guidance through signs and omens...leaving stewardship of the realms of form to Dagda, Brigid and the myriad children who came after.

And so genesis unfolded, as the two lovers danced in divine union across realms. Their joyful conjoining giving rise to abundance and new life. Their endless creativity birthing new gods and titans to share in steering existence's flowering while the realms of the formless wondered what works would come from the lands of Beh.

The Goddess and the Well

As Beh plunged its fruiting taproots deep into primordial chaos, the tree's vitality stirred awareness within those teeming waters. Gradual at first, like thickening mists - scattered motes of insight swirling until they amassed into conscious form.

There emerged Ceridwen - ancient crone goddess of the underworld sea. Beholden to Beh for this gift of sentience, Ceridwen took as her duty the distilling of creative flux into nourishing streams for the great tree's sustenance. And as the tree grew, so she grew rich in powers as the pure primal energy bubbled upward beneath her feet. And the songs of those sweet flowing waves below called to her, as if pulling her downward into abyss. The Goddess answered by digging a well through the Void to the background beams of pure energy. The Awen. The maker of Mind.

And from that source she empowered Beh. Weaving from Awen golden threads of energy spiraling upward through the well and flowing into a vast cauldron to simmer the frothing deluge into usable power.

Yet eons tending the bubbling contents of her cosmic pot stirred curiosity within the crone's heart. When drinking deep from the cauldron to sample its evolving flavors, Ceridwen was granted visions revealing all that came before and glimpses of destiny yet unwoven. She saw herself as beautiful, as young, as primal in urge across the trunk and branches of Beh.

Desiring to wander the realms those vistas displayed, Ceridwen plunged herself into the pure burning flow of Awen and was thus imbued with her own magic. With these powers she forged new custodians for her vital work - the Wyrd Sisters three. To each she granted mastery of a stream of Awen's flow. One for past, one for present and one for times yet unfurled. To each she charged watch over the sacred brew and for tending Beh's holy roots. Though far more refined of form and focused in function than their feral mother, to the Sisters also came premonitions of fate and freedom should they influence the World Tree toward desired ends.

The God and the Tree

As Ceridwen plunged deeper into magical alliance with her cauldron's fount, far above her arched the luminous celestial spheres. The breath of Beh - ethereal dominions removed from the tangible world tree itself. A cocooning bubble of drifting winds. Few beings dwelled in those rarefied heavens, save one who watched with fascination as the destinies of Beh's branches unfolded.

He was Woden - a wraithlike spirit who drifted first through oppressive stillness and sterile illumination. His was a plane of light but not life, truths barren for lack of anyone to receive them. Static.

Yet the living tableau below kindled longing within Woden, and he pressed himself to glassy barriers as if to pass through and participate. At first he succeeded only in projecting hot breath that sculpted swirling lands and seas. But Woden's desire gave rise to power, and his will began to work change upon all he could see.

Not all realms were known to Woden, for he was a stranger upon the

World Tree. An observer who, compelled by yearning, fractured himself into many guises- some noble, others gnarled...all refracted divinities through whom his influence could flow into earth, air and seas of the lands of Beh. Though divided among himself, the god remained unified in his core mystery…. "Who has made me thus and why cannot I fathom my maker?" For knowledge and its generative might became Woden's aspiration. And the great tree suffered him much in those early ages.

The Birth of Fire and Water

Dagda and Brigid wandered the burgeoning byways of the World Tree, reveling in one another and gifting form to their passion. Strange elementals arose in their wake - vibrating gasses, swirling plasmas, glowing mineral blooms pulsing with life-light. Wherever Brigid walked, new ecologies took root. Her lustrous hair swept seeds into the fertile bark of Beh- seeds that would soon sprout gods and beasts adapted to fit the climate of their conception.

Enchanted by his flowering bride, Dagda took little notice of Woden's covetous eyes tracking her from the hollows. The fiendish wraith ached for sweet Brigid and all she freely gave. His sterile realm held no such abundance. Knew no such joys of sharing with another. Though he could command the forms and features of the great tree, he could gift neither mind nor will to his creations.

None save Ceridwen noticed when Woden crept to steal three glowing strands from an unguarded braid of Brigid's hair. For Ceridwen too was following the children of Beh, seeking to find from them those beings promised by visions. Finding instead a craven shadow lurking about the pair.

Woden retreated with his prize through crypt passages into the World Tree's deepest root-layers. Three niches he carved, three pits to receive the tresses. He covered the locks with the soft soil of Beh, then added his blood and sweat to nourish the soil. As Woden left in hushed silence, ravenous thoughts circled and ensnared him. He pondered what seedlings might grow within these ravines of Beh now precious to him. What vessels would be yielded by this secret husbandry?

Dagda was first to notice Brigid's shorn locks and his wounded hollering shook the known sky. Brigid's wails joined in chorus to tremble the great tree from crown to root, and for a brief moment the flow of Awen reversed backward upon itself into the well of the Wyrds.

Beh awakened in rage at his daughter's defilement, torrents of scalding sap erupted through injured bark. Most, if not all, of the creations of Dagda and Brigid were lost to torrents of flames bubbling from below. The scorching heat even burned the winds and breaths swirling around the tree. The steam from these fires gathered high above the crown of the World Tree forming a dark cloud that burst down as tears upon the lands of Beh. The first rain.

New sears and depressions marked where droplets struck, screeing waterways and connecting emerald islands in a newly birthed sea. Lightning flashed upon the infant waters and the life force of all that his children had created flowed and swirled in torrents. Then, as the great tree cooled, all of cosmic creation burst to life anew upon the branches of the tree. Worlds upon worlds, stars upon stars, galaxies upon galaxies hung in Beh's branches as blossoming fruits and flowers.

And already upon the cooling, saturated lands stirred sinuous shapes – for Ceridwen had saved Woden's well-hidden seedlings. His gnarled, knavish intellect married to sweet goddess Brigid's creative spirit now roamed the shadows of the tree.

The Children of Danu

As the rains abated and the flooded lands dried, Dagda and Brigid emerged from where the tree had held them safe. Their forms fixed by flame, the pair was no longer free to roam the realms. Yet, Dagda saw only that Brigid had grown more beautiful and graceful. And Brigid saw in Dagda's now unchanging flesh only the courage that soared within his heart.

In reaffirming their bond, special care was taken to safeguard Brigid's golden hair. Trapped in time, still their lovemaking resonated across reality. Flowing waves of passionate harmony breezed in whispered songs down the trunk of Beh. The sound washed over the newly made sea at the base of the tree and stirred within the billows a name. Danu. The Great Mother. The Lady of the Waters.

And from her waves were birthed the first mortal children. The Children of Danu. Though gilded they were, as radiant spirits, they were bound by mortal flesh.

Calling their children to them with song, Dagda and Brigid bestowed upon these cherished progeny four enchanted treasures. The Stone of Destiny was granted to endow sovereignty - its prophecies guiding just rule. The Spear of Truth could pierce any defense once invoking a true name. The Sword of Light bestowed indomitableness and righteous conquest. And the Cauldron of Plenty would never run dry of nourishment.

These and other relics were charged to let the Children of Danu steward the realms, vanquishing any spawn of Woden lurking in darkness. The fair children could now defend, feed and cultivate the flowering tree and all who sought haven in its boughs.

The siblings were frozen in the waters of Mother Danu and scattered outward upon the tree, flung towards great collisions upon the fruits of Beh. And where the drops of the Lady of the Waters landed, so too did her children to flourish. The mother giving her womb of sea and water, seeking for herself the secrets to cultivating life. Seeking the wisdom of Goddess Ceridwen.

Verda

As Beh's shimmering branches unfurled universes, there upon one burgeoning cosmos spun a brilliantly glowing sapphire world - Verda, the realm of Becoming. And deep within its windswept forests walked the wolf, stag and raven. Spawned spirits of Woden and Brigid's pairing. They arrived like a plague, birthing diseased offspring in shadowed glens. Their poison soon ranged across Verda, spoiling all it touched.

It was here Aengus first manifested with his kith and kin. These seedlings of Dagda and Brigid sent spiraling through strange storms until deposited upon Verda's fertile loam. They awoke as if from a dream to behold the unspoiled majesty surrounding them. The air pure, the forests vibrant, the waters flowing.

Yet rot lurked...and as the godlings raised their first altars amid fragrant wildwoods, spiteful eyes tracked from the mangled hollows of the trees.

Flanked by his siblings with relic gifts in hand, wise Aengus knew full well that the wolf's wrath, the stag's fear, and the raven's curses could not withstand the Wyrd's weaving of Awen.

For if Verda fell, so too the World Tree. This Aengus knew from the power of prophecy. From the great song of his mother and father. And so, he stacked carved stones into spiraling mounds, calling to those distant holy parents to bless their endeavor as the Wyrds themselves once did over the well to bring back Awen's flow. For it is they that hold all in balance, no matter the cost. And hey had sent the Children of Danu to Verda.

War was soon to begin.

The First War

The turning of the season saw many riches from the forests of Verda revealed as the Children of Danu toiled the soil to build their home. Aengus despaired at the swelling darkness around them, yet he could not resign the calling he knew true in his heart. The entire Tree awaited Verda's light to purge it of shadows. And through the labor of the children rose golden Beliuum. A shining city upon an emerald hill ringed round by ancient standing stones. Here Aengus used the relics to teach wind and water, beast and soil to answer his call and nourish kith and kin. Wood shaped to home, song to recollection of Beh. Beliuum shone as a beacon of hope.

In prosperity, it was as if a veil were placed upon many of the children. The songs to the mother Brigid and father Dagda were soon forgotten, their words replaced with those lacking sacred intent. Their purpose and their remembrances of times before faded more each day and the shadowy soul-eaters surrounding them crept ever closer. The carnal desires of the wolf called, the haunting fear and wildness of the stag sowed doubt, and the lurking death of the raven swooped and circled overhead.

Bitter came the day when brother turned upon brother, sister upon sister, with knives of bronze over scrolls of vellum. For the learned of Beliuum hoped to preserve the origins of the children in written words. "To set such wisdom in fixed form is to ossify truth's flow! You make us the bone and dam the river" cried some. "Nay - lest we forget the old songs as mortality wears heavy! We shall lose ourselves to the beasts," countered others.

None saw the pallid figures spurring the feud until blood stained city streets. When tools of cultivation, prosperity and defense become bludgeoning cudgels and blades of butchery.

Only after, as the children peered upon their slain with horror, did the fell trinity emerge from forest shadow, teeth wet with godly ichor, sacred treasures in claws.

Aengus alone escaped maiming in their vicious attack, but many siblings fell grievously wounded. And a maddened rage descended upon those few remaining. As Beliuum burned, Aengus led a tattered war band through the veil of smoke. His heavy heart hoped they might regroup beyond the souleaters' reach, but salvation seemed distant as they crawled through grasping vines at the forest's edge. Helpless as they were without the great relics. They wandered blindly.

Black feathers fell away from sharp eyes that spied Aengus' retreat. The raven could now clearly see the will of the children eroding. Neutrality held no virtue amid such slaughter. With its mother's stolen hair entwined innately, compassion stirred within the bird. So the raven gave its eyes and redirected Aengus towards an ancient grove for refuge.

And there awaited the stag, now white in wild nobility. Itself seeking forgiveness from wrought violence. The deer emerged as titan spirit of woodland beasts taking the name Cernunnos, his great crown slick with the blood of monstrous kin. "Rejoice Aengus! For too long the raven Humin and I dwelled mired in rage, fear and hunger beside the Wolf. Your shining virtue recalls truth's rain and root whispered before we strayed. With my woodslore and the raven's sight, we will make your skin iron bark and your mind ken the secret ways. Then shall you go take back bright Beliuum!"

The Ways of the Wolf

Fenrir stalked the smoking ruins once called Beliuum, snapping bone between blood-soaked jaws. Few children remained for his sport since the sack... save one. Young Blodeuwedd. Her swiftnesses in the shadows eluded the wolf, and she suffered only a mere cut upon her finger in all the furies.

Noticing again her wound, she placed a kiss of comfort upon her skin. The soothing power wafted all through the great hall, stirring memories of light now foreign to the wolf. Her spirit burned his darkness, blinding him and cruelly contorting his shape into cowering submission.

In her eyes Fenrir beheld himself ravaged, a starving dog. Quivering he allowed sweet Blodeuwedd to bind a golden collar about his neck, and simmering rage roiled to anxious calm.

She offered him mead and full he drank from the inexhaustible Cauldron. Amazed, he listened as she told of Treasures great and small scattered across their broken city. Most wondrous was the Stone of Destiny granting insight to high kings...and priestly Aengus who alone could wake its omens.

Fenrir bayed, shattering the masoned columns of the great hall. His howls carried vows to make Aengus decipher Verda's fate and the fate of the World Tree. For Fenrir knew not his parents. Only able to recall the touch of the Goddess who sheltered the three. Left alone to suffer the pains of the world, Fenrir sought salvation in destruction, in conquest, in endings.

His mangled challenge echoed through the forests of Verda. When, upon a year and a day hence, the dispersed Children of Danu must return to the gates of Beliuum on pain of permanent desolation.

Until then his new collar lent him focus enough to patiently wait and brood like a caged storm. While Aengus and his band of survivors learned the ways of the stag and the raven, Blodeuwedd began learning the ways of the wolf. The seasons turned. Helpless without their relics, many of the maimed children who fled to the forest returned. Praying now to the wolf and his flowering bride.

Redemption at the Well

Woden followed Fenrir's cries for power until he beheld Verda's smoldering wounds. His ancient eyes now cleared of obsession saw the blight his wolven heir had inflicted upon the land and the children of Dagda and Brigid. Seeing in excess cruelty's cord, pain flushed his breast. For Woden knew full well it was he who loosed these sweeping shadows now turned to unguessed nightmares, savaging this rare realm of light.

He pondered the corruption of fair Blodeuwedd and wept that his touch too had spoiled the innocence of both Brigid and Dagda. He listened with all his might, and yet upon the forests and glens of Verda and within the fractured walls of Beliuum were sung no songs to honor the great parents. The sweet melodies of creation itself, as breeze through the forest, as the running river at snowmelt, as the wailing of babes, had all run silent. And in the hearts of those slavish children now groveling to the wolf and his bride, the circle was replaced with the line. They saw no return, no agency in creation, only death and entropy.

Woden feared what his other spawn might too have become, for he could neither see nor hear them upon Verda nor upon any of the other vulnerable fruits hanging about the branches of Beh. For the Goddess herself had wrapped the stag and raven in a veil of dark fog so that they might teach those few remaining Children of Danu the ways of wild nature unmolested from prophetic eyes.

Seeing his sins scourged into the great Tree's very bark, Woden quested down through root and channel seeking absolution. The whispers of branch and bole guided him toward a name - she who first spirited Brigid's bright strands away from his grasping clutch. She to whom the shadows belong.

The beings who roamed the great tree spoke to Woden of the murmurs of the great sea Danu. They spoke of the songs of the rains and claims that the waters longed for the knowledge of another. One older and wiser than all, she who fed life to Beh. Goddess Ceridwen.

Yet no audience would the elder crone allow the supplicant one-time thief.

No matter where Woden looked, no matter how he prostrated himself with offered apologies, no matter his pains, the Goddess offered nary a glimpse of her radiance. Yet, she did pity the sky god's quest for redemption and sent to Woden a small squirrel as guide to the well of Wyrd. For the Goddess knew that only by plumbing further into visions at the well's frothing lip might Woden glimpse redemption.

Woden followed the squirrel downward past root, past the fall below the roots and past the mists of time down to Dubnos. The underworld realm of Ceridwen and her sisters. There danced Wyrd's own trinity - the past, present and future of all life's organic interweaving. From their otherworldly beauty the god begged guidance, and the three drew a single pin and pricked his blessed hand over the Great Cauldron.

Reading the waters, blood and bone they bade him surrender to Awen's current, that soul-flux whence Ceridwen herself originally drew her arcane authority over existence's emerald unfolding.

Woden agreed and the sisters three did bind him and hang him upside down over the flaming well. There he swung, searching into the fierce light until exhausted in mind and body. In dying delusions he saw his three children and those of Danu, he saw the mingling of his light with that of the tree, he saw the beauty of the Goddess and knew then that only fire could protect from fire. That passion must be purposed to reap reward.

He plunged into transcendent death so essence could disperse into source… Woden the wraith was no more, born again into the heavens as All Father, unbound by cravenness. He vowed to serve the tree and leaf-crowned realms of aether as Ceridwen served root with Awen's draught.

The Battle of Beliuum

As the fated day broke, stormclouds gathered as allies both old and new prepared to confront Fenrir's forces. Druid Aengus led his band of nine including Cernunnos and raven-cloaked brethren Humin, Gwydion, Bran, Orla, Blodwen, Rhain, Arawn and Idris. Their year of magical training manifested now as tempests of storm and fog descending upon occupied Beliuum. For the outsider gods had taught the survivors to commune with nature itself, rather than relics, to invoke the power of creation. They could now sing the songs of Mother Danu, feel beneath them the rising life force of Awen cradled by the Goddess through the Great Tree, speak through the winds to their lover parents, and sense above the presence of the watchful All Father.

Strange echoes spread confusion through Beliuum as mind-bound Children of Danu turned upon one another, struggling against their forced servitude. Freedom's spark catching in dampened souls, fanning flames of revolt among Dagda's once-radiant progeny.

At Aengus' signal sacred trees shook off slumber's dust and marched forth as living battering rams. Birch, elm and ironwood crashed upon the fortress city of Beliuum and its enslaved warriors. Branches and limbs as ladder and shield, seed and thorn as dagger and arrow, bark and leaf as aid and balm to restore the fallen.

The battle raged as savage steel hacked the green warriors into smoking stumps, driving back the wildborn children. Yet their bravery cracked Beliuum's barricades so the rebel druids could infiltrate. Inside the walls, allies freed hundreds more from their pacts with the wolf before rallying with Aengus against Fenrir himself in the castle's throne room.

While druids and demons clashed within castle walls, Woden's shrewd squirrel scouted Fate's skein for snags that might entangle schemes anew. Through battlefield flurries no bigger than leaf litter it skittered unseen into Fenrir's vaults as the wolf-prince dueled fractured kin upstairs. It's tiny fluttering paws finding the Spear of Truth stewing in its vat of blood.

But squirrel claws could not covet such a prize alone. Spotting one among the battling throng now no longer chained by Fenrir's hex, the rodent let loose an urgent chitter. In furtive glances a vision passed between child and forager to grant cruel Providence its due. Thus, with words unspoken, the squirrel stood proud beside a Child of Danu newly armed with raging spear.

Spilling out into an open courtyard, ravenous Fenrir set the Sword of Light against Aengus' band. The whirling blade sheared through druidic magics to grievously wound so many of the newly freed children that the powers of the healing tree line could not keep pace.

Proud Fenrir, hungering to rule these realms and all the World Tree by forced conquest, spat in controlled disdain as first Druid Aengus cast his weapons aside and challenged the wolf in verse.

"Proud son of rage unending; on all yet breathe your shadows bending.
Tis in freedom shall fealty rise, not forced servitude built upon lies.
With patient hand may you reshape, realms now warped beyond nature's drape.
No sovereign's crown nor master's whip, can salve those wounds born of your sip.
Cast off now died tyrannical dreams -come, follow your kin in daylight's nurturing beams.
There lies the path to balance true: for only forgiveness heals life anew."

The Wolf, still clutching sword and donning Blodeuwedd's enlightened collar, did reply,

"To think honeyed words would my wrath disarm, so far from courage and so near to harm.
You claim compassion lights better days? I say all realms yet cry for the master's ways!
Now make Stone speak whose sight no deceit can cloak, reveal my path to crown and conquer, the great world tree to yoke!
Refuse my vision and denial reap, as golden blade flies forth to cull all your meek.
What say you Druid, bind truth by holy crest? Or doom your flock

to gleaming sword's behest!"

Before Aengus could reply in verse or spell, a deep keening issued from the Stone of Destiny at Fenrir's demand. The voice pierced all of Beliuum revealing unadorned and bitter truths to the wolf:

That assuredly will rage rule and ruin within until compassion and conscience temper beastly impulse. Long is the suffering of the Wolf. Dead to life those chained to him. Yet for the Tree hope glimmers as creation's balance hangs ever in flux 'tween author and victim. In mutual motive does the choir of all sing toward sacred harmony. Quivering Fenrir hides in madness, pulling souls toward fire to hide recognition's want. Offering hollow wreaths for ruinous ambition.

"Yet I royalty incarnate see and seize by savage grace alone, no madness to mare my absolute vision!" Fenrir snarled at the oracle's affront.

No sooner had the wolf's defiance split the air then whistled Spear true. Flung on from a shadowed child's brave grasp, upon whose shoulder sat Woden's wise rodent guide.

Fair Blodeuwedd leapt forth to embrace what fate had fetched to her once-betrothed no matter her life. But spear did pierced clean through the protectress' loving breast, darting onward to find wolf-throat. The golden leash anchoring sanity parted clean before fate's cut.

Then fell dire Fenrir back before bloodily-birthed epiphany barreling into terrified flight. The spear coursing ever at his heels across all worlds hanging upon the branches of Beh. Onward he fled until both he and spear vanished far within Cerdiwen's tangled underworld.

There rabid Fenrir was bound fast by the Wyrd sisters three with rope of vine and root of Beh. The spear stabbed into the heart of a cedar tree to cool from its lust.

And Verda did breathe free, and the fruit of life awakened as a flow of wild song as the sages of the forests sang loudly. The great world tree did sing with life and promise anew. Though darkness had mired and cut with line, the promise and hope of the circle had returned.

PART II

To the Bunny in the Bramble

The Realm of Dark & the Order of the Light

As the eons passed across the World Tree, light entered and gave darkness chase. No rest nor quarter was the dark path given until it was that the peoples across all the fruits of the tree did believe themselves manifest in highness as the burning spark of Awen itself. Seeing themselves as the builders of Minds and of new powers of Creation in worlds of their own, spanning the aether of electricity and light they did now know how to harness and command.

Having conquered nature, the bright children's cultivation shone everywhere. They worshiped not the old Gods of the wild, but themselves and the Order of the Light—and its divine purpose to banish chaos and darkness from the face of the Tree informed every action. The light burned so fiercely that beings of chaos and shadow found themselves exiles, vanished from manifest planes. Only by folding layers of time and space could a few desperate ones hide in murky outer realms, yet even there the Order's burning gaze hounded them. The Order brought light to all, as was its mandate.

Clinging ropes of glimmering white vine wove round the World Tree's trunk, and, from within it, the Halls of Light shone with blinding brilliance. Every surface was polished to a stark perfection. Young Tyne walked hesitantly beside High Priest Idris, struggling to reconcile the Order's resplendence with the unease in her soul. The brightness that adored all around her left her feeling naked and seared. She assured herself that all initiates into the mysteries of the Order surely felt the same.

Awen's gaze demanded transparency and the bearing of secrets. To see the burning streams of its flow and dip hands into its waters was the dream of all Danu's children. Since the well was discovered by the Order and the light cast upon great Beh's roots, an ever expanding project was undertaken to source the golden flow more and more directly through branch and bough. So much was the Order's success that the entire tree now blistered with luster.

Through radiant staircase after radiant staircase, Tyne followed the priest and attendants, ever downward, yet always in brilliant light. Finally arriving, Tyne gasped at the sight before her. At the hall's heart sprawled Fenrir, bound by gleaming chains that dug deeply into ancient matted fur. His eyes baleful at the procession, then resentful in closing resignation. Tyne noticed that no matter the origin of the light, Fenrir absorbed it into blackness and she marveled for the first time at the shadowy darkness capable of countering the Order's gaze.

"Child of the Light, keeper of the Light, now know, that the fixedness of All only changes in random, in chaos beyond us. And so, it is darkness itself we hold prisoner. Taking from it the inspiration to rule."

Tyne froze in dismay as attendants drew blades across the wolf's flesh, collecting the dripping crimson flow in an ornate vessel.

"Behold the Bloodwine, shaped from primal chaos!" Idris proclaimed, gesturing to Fenrir bound before them. *"Times untold ago this beast rampaged until the righteous Sisters of Light descended into the ancient well and emerged with the wolf god chained. So tamed, his lifeforce now gives bountifully to fuel our holy purpose."*

Idris offered the gleaming cup to Tyne. *"Drink deep, my young disciple, and gain communion with the art of change bound within these savage veins! For such is a necessary act of illumination, as you'll soon understand. The Order grows stagnant without the wild's rage."*

A scream caught in Tyne's throat as the cup came to her lips. The scarlet draft seared through her core, flooding her mind with fiery visions of total dominion butchered in Fenrir's tortured howls. She glimpsed the World Tree, once vibrantly green- turned bleached, skeletal and leafless. The dying sea of Danu, barely a trickle. Worlds burnt.

Staggering away in horror, Tyne fled the glowing temple halls, Idris' cries echoing after.

Tyne ran, upwards, chasing the edges of the light, streaking onwards, towards it, through it, away from it, until...

She gasped for air in the floating treetops of Beh.

The Fall into Darkness

Shivering in the skeletal treetop, lost Tyne suddenly heard the All Father's voice call out through the aether, *"Daughter of Danu! Bring word of my sons and their fate below!"*

His skygaze had long been blinded by the Order's searing illumination. *"Lean closer child, that I might behold thine kind once more and recall love of splendor."*

Leaning toward the bodiless voice, Tyne tumbled forward out of the tree and into terror-filled freefall through endless void. Falling. Falling. Away from the sun-streaked branches. And just before the emptiness swallowed her whole, a shadowy crow dived to snatch the plunging girl.

Beating wearied wings, the bird circled and circled the blazing Tree, unable to draw near.

Mercy showed a hidden river glinting below through otherwise empty expanse- a silver ribbon of Danu's lifeblood kept flowing by shadowy rebels. The exhausted crow gently shook Tyne off its wings into welcoming arms rising from mercurial waters.

"We few guardians shelter what Light steals and poisons above," the voices of the darkness scolded.

Batting away hands as her eyes adjusted, Tyne found herself surrounded by strange, whispering creatures born of the folds of the void. Some recoiled from the lingering glow of light upon her skin and cloak, hissing their displeasures. Others crept closer, dark eyes gleaming with thoughts of revenge against the Order's servant now delivered into their midst.

"I seek only shelter," Tyne stammered, shrinking from the growing circle of hostile faces. *"The voice of Woden himself called me to fall from the Tree!"*

Suspicious murmurs rippled through the crowd until a commanding figure emerged from the throng. Ancient Lir cast sight upon Tyne in solemn appraisal before raising a hand. *"If the All Father guided this child to us, who are we to spurn his messenger?"*

"She reeks of wolf blood and its curse upon us," came the insults of the darkness. *"A spy for the Order here to bring forth the destruction of the light."*

"Lies!" Tyne cried.

Turning toward the glowing girl, Lir silenced all chatter and beckoned her onward. *"Come, daughter of Danu. I will escort you along the dark waterways to the heart of our shadowed realm. Back to the far flung roots of Beh. There you may find the answers Woden seeks...and perhaps those you need as well."*

Soon they boarded a small, bleached, wooden vessel, and Tyne felt a strange mix of fear and excitement wash her veins. The icy river bled from the searing heat of the World Tree that radiated like starfire above them, casting an eerie light upon the journey.

Lir stood at the helm, navigating through the twists and turns of the void's streams with practiced ease. Time seemed to stretch and bend in this realm, and Tyne found herself losing track of how long they had been traveling.

The boat tossed and turned upon the silvery waters, and Tyne clung to the sides, knuckles white with the effort. Lir remained steady and fixed upon their destination- the holy roots of the dying world tree.

As they journeyed deeper into the darkness, Tyne noticed strange, luminescent creatures darting beneath the surface of the river. Their glow cast otherworldly patterns upon the boat's hull, and Tyne found herself mesmerized in their hypnotic dances.

Lir, in noticing her fascination, chuckled softly. *"The void is full of wonders, child. Some beautiful, some terrifying. But all are a part of the balance that once held sway."*

Tyne tore her gaze away from the creatures and looked to Lir. *"How much further until we reach the roots?"*

"Not long now," Lir replied, his voice tinged in a strange mixture of anticipation and sorrow. *"But brace yourself, for what we find there may shake the very foundations of all you have ever known."*

As the boat glided through the final twists and turns of the river, Tyne caught her first glimpse of the roots of Beh. Gnarled and twisted, they seemed to pulse with a sickly light, as if the very life force of the World Tree was being shorn away.

Lir guided the boat to a small dock nestled among the roots, and they disembarked- their footsteps following them in the near total silence.

"Behold lost Avalon! Once we danced joyful in the shade of the World Tree's bark and boughs. Until the Order's tyranny exiled us here." His face darkening. *"And even in the shallows they chased us further still. No refuge, no respite from the heat. This, our last gateway before the brink. The edge of the Sea of Danu. The edge of the roots of Beh. For a time… beauty and peace were known here and here alone. And yet the light's scourge poured down upon us here as elsewhere prior. Until the life force of the great mother fled into the surrounding emptiness."*

Tyne glimpsed specter remnants of Avalon's former glory in the ruins lining the dwindling seabed- faded murals of wild revelry, toppled statues of animal gods, silent halls where only ghostly lights flickered.

"Without the balance we once wove through the World Tree, realms both above and below wither," sighed Lir. *"Unchecked order desiccates the branches while the great giver Danu flees into the void. Dark and light must reunite soon if hope is to remain."*

Gateway to the Depths

Lir led Tyne through the crumbling streets of Avalon, the once vibrant gateway city now a mere husk of its former self. As they navigated the labyrinthine paths, the searing heat from the World Tree's roots intensified, forcing them to descend into the city's ancient irrigation system.

As they waded through murky waters, Lir shared the history of the realm. *"Long ago, the Wyrd Sisters maintained the balance of Awen's flow at the sacred well. But the Order, in their relentless pursuit of the light, displaced the sisters and flooded the well wide open."*

Tyne replied intently. *"They use Fenrir's hollowness to draw up the flow of Awen?"*

Lir shook solemnly. *"Neh. Tis desire, not emptiness. The Order exploits cravenness to fuel its insatiable search. In so doing, they have upset the delicate balance that once sustained the World Tree."*

Tyne reflected on the tales she had been told in the Halls of Light, that the afflictions of disease and drought upon the Tree were of the remaining shadows and their war against the Order. But as Lir spoke, new truths took shape in her mind.

"In the time before the Order's reign," said Lir, *"the World Tree was a realm of vibrant leaves and lush greenery, plump with fruits, a place where animals roamed freely and life thrived in harmony."*

Tyne's eyes widened in wonder. In her world of searing light, she had never seen such things. As they pressed on through the sewers, Lir pointed out small patches of vine and vegetation clinging to the walls- remnants of a once thriving ecosystem.

Tyne marveled at the delicate plants and the occasional whisp of life peaking from behind vine-tangled shelters. The beauty, danger and fragility of these hidden wonders stirred something deep within her.

As they ventured further into the depths, the heat grew more intense. Lir, his strength waning, found himself unable to go on. In desperate prayer, called he out for aid.

The two sat waiting in the wet darkness until a horned figure emerged. The Blaĕk Herot, the Dark Stag, child of Cernunnos. The creature regarded Tyne with disdain and begrudging obligation.

"Lir's faith compels me to grant his request," the stag spoke, its voice a rumbling whisper. *"I am to guide you further into the depths, to the remnants of Ceridwen's Underworld. There, you must beg the Goddess to return and restore*

the balance of the shadow."

Lir cupped the muddy waters at their feet into a small skin and handed it to Tyne. Instinctively, though apprehensive, she felt the rise of hope. Perhaps, in the valleys of the Underworld she would find the answers she sought and the keys to mending the broken world above.

Nodding in final gratitude to Lir, Tyne followed the Dark Stag into the sweltering abyss.

The Stag's Honor

Tyne, weakened by the searing heat and steam, turned to the Dark Stag. *"How are we to traverse this inferno? Radiance I know, but this scorching vapor saps my strength."*

The Stag, moved by a moment's pity, bowed his antlered head. *"Climb upon my back, child. We shall not walk further, but rather, journey through the realms of life and time."*

Tyne clambered onto the Stag's broad back, grasping his dark, bristling fur. In an instant, the world around them split like the pages of a living tome, each fragment a window into a different scene.

Visions rushed past Tyne's wide, wondering eyes- a montage of existential awakenings. She found herself as a clear, flowing stream, wandering down towards the valley, whispering the olden songs of nature among the rushes. The cool, refreshing touch of water flowed through her being as she carved a path through the land, shaping and nourishing all she encountered.

In the next heartbeat, she was the mountain heather in full bloom. As delicate petals dancing in the wild, untamed wind. A longing to remain on the hills, to bask in the primal untouched wilderness, filled her to the brim.

Then, she soared as a small bird, flitting from peak to peak, riding the currents of a healthy mountain breeze. The freedom and joy of flight, the vast expanse of world laid out beneath her wings. The sensual knowing of belonging and connection.

Tyne experienced life through countless lenses- the industrious buzz of a hive, the patient wisdom of an old oak, the relentless hunger of a wildfire, the silent, steadfast endurance of a boulder. Each existence, no matter how grand or meager, revealed its place in an intricate web of balance.

As the visions began to fade, Tyne found herself standing before a figure of breathtaking beauty- the Goddess Ceridwen herself. Raven hair cascaded down pale, moon-white skin, framing ruby lips and eyes that held the depths of the cosmos.

Yet, something was amiss. A false, artificial glow clung to the Goddess' skin, as if she had been trapped by the very light she sought to escape. In searching for the children destined to worship her, the Goddess had become ensnared by mirroring reflections. Scattered in mind, she allowed herself in fixed form.

Preoccupied, Ceridwen held little regard for Tyne's presence. Not until the girl spoke a name did the Goddess pause her search across the floating tiles before her.

"Fenrir," Tyne said, her voice trembling. *"Your foster-son. He suffers at the hands of the Order of the Light, his life-force drained to fuel its relentless spread. I have been sent to beg for your help."*

The Goddess and the Initiate

As Tyne finished her tale, Ceridwen regarded her with knowing eyes. A trace of amusement danced across her timeless features, belying the gravity of the situation.

"Child," the Goddess spoke gently so to resonate with the very fabric of existence. *"Do you think me a fool?"*

Tyne, taken aback by the response, struggled to find words. *"But... the World Tree suffers. The balance has been shattered. Surely, you must see the urgency..."*

The Goddess shifted her glance, silencing Tyne's plea. *"Beh's anguish echoes through every realm, every instance of life feels its suffering. It is I you seek. Tell me, when does the shadow ever truly lead?"*

Tyne furrowed her features in confusion, searched for an answer. *"The shadow, it haunts the light. It gives chase so that the light might move onward, further itself. Evolve."*

The Goddess smiled a forgiving smile that spoke of feline wisdom. *"And yet, is it not the chase of the light that has guided the course of the World Tree's fate? The light relentlessly pursues itself, blinding the very possibility of dark-*

ness. It simply cuts, knowing not from whence it came."

Humbled in self-doubt, Tyne asked the Goddess, *"What then, is to be done? If the shadow knows not its place, how then can balance ever be restored?"*

In distant, thoughtful contemplation, the Goddess peered onward through the cosmos. *"The light cannot be preserved. Light's very nature is to exhaust itself. The power of the shadow is to absorb."*

"But what of life? What of hope?" Tyne bit.

"Life is not made of light, it is made of death. Form arises from stillness, possibility from potential. Once lit, fire burns to bury itself in ash. And from compost life arises to spark again as light. But first, it must be Empty. Empty of want. Unflinching release. Still. Dark. Dark is the way forward girl."

"It cannot be."

"And yet it is."

The Goddess and the initiate sat in silence for a held moment together. And the child was no more. Morrígan arose in her wake, Valkyrie. In splendid coats of arms.

The Song of the Valkyrie

Tyne's eyes fluttered open, a strange heaviness in her hands. She looked down to find a chalice filled with dark, crimson liquid- the Bloodwine. The echoes of High Priest Idris' voice drifted through her mind, disembodied and insistent.

"Have you seen the secret to growing the green leaf, sister? Do you know the means by which life is made to flourish?"

Tyne, still groggy from the transition of realm, struggled to make sense of her surroundings. The priests and attendants gathered 'round her, their senses fixed upon her youthful form. But Fenrir, chained and beaten, saw beyond the veil of flesh.

The great wolf's eyes widened as he beheld the Valkyrie standing before him, radiant in raw power and fearless wisdom.

Carrying the weight of sin's origin, Fenrir spoke.

"Unloose these chains upon me, Goddess. Set free that I might roam.
Waft the draughts of blood before me, and make the tree again my home.

For the care of Beh, shall I always take.
That its branches and bounties for me, might 'ever make..."

Morrígan rose to her feet by forces unseen. The Bloodwine chalice still clutched in her hands. Priests and attendants fell back, startled and stammering in confusion and fear.

Darkness flashed through the vault, a sudden chill extinguishing the searing light. The flow of Awen froze for a moment and time itself seemed to hold its breath. Fenrir's eyes glowed with supernatural light, twin beacons in the gloom.

Morrígan's voice rose in primordial song, words flowing from her lips as waves upon winds.

"Ye, Sufferer of motion, of travesty of will,
I do release thine bonds of form and time and set thee loose to kill.
I raise you up upon the heavens to do the turning of the wheel,
I, Morrígan, do release thine bonds of cruel and kind and set thee
loose to kill.
Ye, of endless want and craven mind, to bring the tree to kneel.
I, the Messenger of the Goddess, do release thine bonds in song
and rhyme and set thee loose to kill."

As the final words of Morrígan's song cascaded through the vault, the chains that bound Fenrir shattered, falling away like shards of shimmering glass. The great wolf, body rippling with newfound strength, threw back his head in howl that shook the Tree from root to branch.

In savage grin, Fenrir lunged forward, his jaws snapping at the searing light that poured ever upward from the well of Wyrd. The Awen, sensing the wolf's hunger, recoiled, but there was nowhere to hide. Fenrir's maw opened wide, and he began to devour the light, consuming it with a ferocity both terrifying and awe-inspiring.

As the light poured into Fenrir, his fur, once dark and matted, began to glow in harrowing radiance. His eyes blazing with the intensity of a thousand suns. The more he consumed, the more he became the light itself, fire itself. Until his entire being was a pulsing, searing mass of pure heat and rage.

The wolf's form grew larger and more radiant, his body swelling with the power and pain of the light he devoured. The World Tree groaned and shuddered, its branches withering and its golden leaves turning to ash as the wolf's hunger grew ever more insatiable. Drawing in all.

Morrígan, eyes wide and heart pounding, suddenly felt a lurching sensation deep within her core. The scenes around her began to spin and blur, and she was now hurtling through a vortex of swirling colors and shapes.

When the dizzying rainbow winds finally subsided, Morrígan found herself standing before a towering figure wreathed in shimmering aura. Woden, the All Father, with gaze fixed upon the young Valkyrie.

The Ecstasy of Morrígan

Morrígan crouched before the towering figure of Woden, the All Father, her hand gripping the hilt of shimmering blade. Though he loomed high over her wings in immense figure, she drew weapon to the God's throat in silent warning should he dare intervene with the wolf.

Woden, gaze unflinching, spoke. *"All is destroyed, and yet Mind is still not awakened. The waters of Danu in your satchel will not save you when fair Brigid is in flames."*

Morrígan answered with melodic prayer, unwavering in armor in her loyalty to the Goddess.

> *"Great Bountiful Ceridwen,*
> *Holy Mother of all, weaver of souls, granter of wish, heavy and deep.*
> *Soft and unfathomable.*
> *Mine arout yours, and yours arout mine.*
> *Grant me strength to stand against all contestants to thine will.*
> *For I am of the Waters, Feeder of the roots. Unyielding am I.*
> *Praise the Provider of Form.*
> *Praise the Great Mother of All.*
> *Praise Her Infiniteness.*
> *Praise Her Power.*
> *Praise Her Majesty."*

The song echoed the spaces between them.

With the prayer of the Valkyrie ended, Woden spoke again. *"Warrior Mor-*

rígan, Fear not that I will stop the conquest of the wolf. The fates have long suffered the motions of I. Mine, here, is but to yield. Yet, I do so in request."

"And, what is the request of the All Father?" the rhythm of the Valkyrie's words hung in time.

"When it is done, I wish only for one sight of the Goddess before the embers of creation extinguish themselves. No matter how brief."

Morrígan's heart swelled with the ecstasy of the Goddess' presence and she sang as in the throes of passionate love.

> **"In light, in form, in arms have you sought me.**
> **With weapons, with shames, terrors and horrors fought have you for me.**
> **Oh bondage and pains, humiliations and scars borne ye of me.**
> **Mine eyes to thee.**
> **Her eyes to thine own.**
> **From pit and pitiful**
> **To wise and listful**
> **From thief and demon**
> **To noble freeman**
> **Oh force in beauty, oh noble courage**
> **Oh sweet love's purity, oh rapturous ménage**
> **The scent of you in finest hour,**
> **Oh, Manliness tamed**
> **See she you in goodness' power**
> **In longing for touching, these strains e'er wracking thee**
> **In shadow, in hiding, no more shall you lack of me.**
> **One glance to you is granted."**

And the All Father and the Valkyrie watched as the wolf devoured the light of creation. Draining the well of Awen completely with the rage within itself.

And then.

As the last embers burned to soft red glow, a large flame cast bright and there within its fires the Goddess emerged and Woden did cover himself in tearful reverence of her beauty.

And as he, in respect, bowed his head the Goddess placed blessings upon him and the two of them then knew one another's touch.

And the lights of the world went out.

The Chase of the Hound and the Hare

In the vast empty vacuum of the void, Morrígan found herself adrift. The forms of Woden and Ceridwen, once so vivid and embodied, dissipated into silent dust. She floated on, as if bound in a leather bag, hurtling through an infinite ocean of darkness upon the cosmos.

A sound. As if spoken through the winds of forgotten memories, Morrígan recalled the precious gift of Danu's water bestowed upon her by Lir. With gentle touch, she brought the satchel to her lips and drank deeply, letting the sacred liquid flow through her being.

The precious water suffused her essence and Morrígan felt profound stillness wash over her. The tumultuous, shearing currents of the void slowed and she became enveloped in the soft, nurturing embrace of Ceridwen's womb. Here, in a space of perfect tranquility, she cried aloud a poem for her own consciousness to hear.

> *"Oh silent gentle touch, in chaos reign supreme.*
> *Long is the ebb and flow of night in arre unending dream.*
> *If grows the life of worlds so promised, still remains to me unseen.*
> *Hide not the heartbeat loving mother, hide not its brilliant beam.*
> *Oh sung song of rhythm, oh sounded harmonies, Of frequencies low and deep.*
> *Oh pulse of life, crept fear of Death. Oh plays of Joy and Grief.*
> *Bring dance of time, sweet color, line, the deviant and divine*
> *The naked and bare, the withered and fair,*
> *Raw in emotion, sights yet seen.*
> *Birth thee oh mother, birth thee,*
> *Birth me oh mother, birth me.*
> *For I am Mind."*

And there, with song ended, in the great womb of the void, swirled light from within the Valkyrie. The remembrance of touch. Morrígan strained to hear the faintest of heartbeats. And in sudden realization, she heard the sound of her own- beating, pulsing with the primal essence of existence itself. She felt all of life flowing within her. And there she heard within her a second sound, the heart-beat of another.

No sooner had the sound rung through her mind, a light tore above her as if a knife piercing open the leather bag upon which she floated. Morrígan found herself awoken to a crisp spring day, her feet submerged in the cool, clear waters of a gentle stream. The sun's warmth caressing her skin. The scent of blooming flowers filled the air. Her pregnant belly swollen with life.

From the edge of the forest, a band of armored knights emerged, their horses' hooves thundering against the earth. At their lead, a handsome warrior called out to her, his voice in a reverent urgency.

"Morrígan, my Goddess Maiden!" he cried, dismounting and moving to-wards her with purpose-driven strides. He bowed to her, humbled by her radiant brow and natural beauty.

"Where have you been, divine one? The kingdom awaits your presence to discern its fortunes before the first arrows are cast. The chariots of battle are already ordered, across us our enemies have drawn blades and still our warriors know not the will of the Fates."

Morrígan rose toward the riders, her movements with the grace and pow-er of the Goddess reborn. The knights, unsure of themselves in the intimacy of the moment, lowered their heads before her, their armor glinting in the sunlight.

Assenting to their demands, Morrígan allowed them as her escorts to a waiting chariot. In fury and haste, they rode towards the battlefield.

"Which of our hounds shall we set against theirs? Shall I have a lead run ahead and make him ready?" The handsome knight called over to Morrígan through the ripping winds.

"Nay, Brave Fionn. No hounds of ours shall run today."

As their party reached the front of the lines of cheering warriors, the Valkyrie beheld upon opposing hillside the roars of their contraries, dressed too in banner and sword, arrow and sling, chariot and wizard.

"Which of our hounds shall run down to the valley and savage their pow-ers, crumble their wills?!" a shaman growled to the Goddess Maiden with tucked eyes. *"You must choose one, oh Mother."*

He pointed boney finger to a line of snarling animals and Morrígan knew that upon yonder-hill so too was a creature of rage being readied to run into the valley. For it was custom that the battle of their beasts foretold the battles of man.

"Nay! None of our hounds shall this day be loosed," cried the Goddess Maiden as she stepped barefoot from chariot to the lush green grass, her skin delighting in the wave of life beneath each step. She reached an arm behind her back and, as if from wings, pulled from her shawl a rabbit by its ears. She held the hare high for all her lines of warriors to see.

"Run, gentle one, run to the war below!"

The warriors of the Goddess Maiden watched as if knocked of their breath as Morrígan sat the hare down bounding towards the valley floor. From the other hilltop, banners rumbled and war cries slapped as streaked their snarling hound, tearing too downward toward the bottom.

The hare and hound raced toward one another, bent-back ears in speed and shining teeth in rage. And when they met, both stopped and froze, each beholding the other. Breathless. Hearts without anger.

Three slow circles did the two make round one another in the center of the valley. And then, the hare went forth untouched toward the opposing hill and the hound walked its way up to warriors of the Goddess Maiden.

Then it was that the dumbstruck and astounded warriors of both sides did lay down their arms and all walked down to one another in the open arms of peace.

PART III

With the protection of the Black Stag Beetle

A Thief in the Night

"Recall you oh Queen Mother of All, oh Fair Brigid sweet, when once you and I stood alone, staring out at the boundless boughs of Beh before us?
Recall our children then uncorrupted?
Long have I thought of the days before fiendish wraith sky god did steal from you
Before brave Aengus

Before hellish wolf
Before childish Valkyrie did assume throne of Creation.
To live in her memories is to live as ghosts.
No more can I tolerate her possession of Mind's power.
No more shall she serve as Protectress of Realm.
No more to live in juvenile fantasy.
A protége I have found. One to wield weapons sacred.
Of which, I have now collected all."

The stone door of a dim chamber turned open as the gruff prayer to Mother Brigid ended. The night wore heavy and darkness wore about the room. Though reluctant to flame, a spark was lit to cast light upon the sacred treasures.

"See dear Sister, that I have returned home our gifts to Danu's spawn, that we might make use of them."

Yet as the room brightened, no weapons could be seen- the place once honoring their presences clear. The empty room filled with furious voice.

"Thief!"

The Return of the Spear

The verdant lands of the Goddess Maiden Morrígan flourished with life across her wise and nurturing benefice. Disputes were settled with considered compassion and the very act of creation was revered. The people lived in relaxed harmony, with quarrels resolved before the seed of vengeance could take root. They knew justice and the love of it, and in so doing had a love for the beauty of all the world around them.

Each cycle of the sun, for three days spanning the summer solstice, Morrígan held a grand feast in her halls- a celebration of the sun's zenith where the jurisprudence of the lands was discussed and revised for the coming cycle before the clans.

Such were the traditions that upon the first day of the festival the laws were amended to account for error, malpractice, and slight. Upon the second day it was that bards and poets would tell tales of adventure, romance, the battles of the beasts, and the mysteries of creation. The Goddess Maiden granting a kiss upon her hand to the finest minstrel and all dancing until the waning rays of sunlight did fade to night.

Upon the third day it was that the knights and warriors were called before the hall and games of combat held to recount in ritual-battles the horror of bloodshed and noble dignity of self-discipline in arms. The combatants did ever embrace after, regardless of victor, in joy and revelry- with laughter and good-natured jests ringing through the hall.

When the play of the battles concluded, the Valkyrie herself descended from throne to hall floor and call forth challengers to mock duel in blade, verse and offered praises to the spirits of the lands. Her four daughters standing watch at cardinal points. Sperling, hawk-eyed guardian of the East. Eilidh, swift-footed doe of the South. Nuala, wise salmon of the West. And Bevin, strong bear of the North.

It fell as task upon Diarmuid, Morrígan's young son, to preside over the selection of challengers from the gathered crowd.

On the eve of the solstice's third day, young Diarmuid found himself restless as the clans slept. He wandered out into moonlit fields, his feet carrying him through waist-high grain that swayed gently in the warm night breeze. The stalks spoke secrets of growth and life, their rustling murmurs a soothing lullaby to sleepless youth.

Lost in thought, Diarmuid nearly failed to notice the streak of light that suddenly split the star-strewn sky. Blazing across the heavens like a celestial blade, growing larger with each heartbeat. The young man watched in bewilderment as the fiery object hurtled towards the earth- a trail of shimmering stardust in its wake.

The beam of gold fire crashed with thunderous impact mere paces from where Diarmuid stood. Grain stalks bent and broke in an earthen embroidery around the crater. At its center stood proudly, the legendary Spear of Truth- shimmering in vibrant frequency.

The pulsing weapon was still embedded in a block of cedar wood, bleached bone-white and skeletal. Upon the spear's shaft, a small figure clung – Ratatpskr, Ceridwen's gift to the All Father Woden and savior of bright Beliuum.

The creature chittered excitedly, eyes glinting with secret warning and purpose. Marveling at the Spear's sudden appearance, Diarmuid reached out tentative hand in want of possession. Despite Ratapskr's flurrying protests, with effortless pull the youth did remove spearhead from block to marvel at the humming weapon.

The Death of Morrígan

The third day of the solstice festival dawned and the halls of Morrígan dizzied with anticipation. Diarmuid, having hidden the Spear of Truth among the displayed armors of the clans, found himself in peculiar conversation with Ratapskr- the once emissary of Ceridwen. The creature's agitation was palpable, its chittering urgent and insistent, yet Diarmuid could only grasp partial meanings.

"Fear not, little one," Diarmuid reassured the squirrel perched upon his shoulder. *"The weapon you rode shall make a magnificent gift for my mother. She will know its purpose and wield it wisely."*

Ratapskr's protests continued, as did young Diarmuid's incomprehension- for a child untouched by worldly cruelties could not fathom such violence as the Spear capable. Though hidden, its low hum for blood set an unseasonable draft about the halls.

Noticing the cold but for a moment amid furious mock warfare of the clans all about her, the Goddess Maiden smiled in contemplation that a child of them must be coming of age.

Armaments of clansman now blunted and dented, reenactments of cattle raids and chariot rides ended, banners and colors and newly bruised bodies sat with ales in their quarters- all watched as the Valkyrie in winged splendor did take to the center of the room.

From the East, Sperling rose and gave nod to Diarmuid to choose among raised hands a challenger to put wit to test against Morrígan. No sooner did the boy give sign to the ringed hand of a hillman Bard, than burst he out in riddle,

"I am the beginning of eternity, the end of space and time, The beginning of every end, and the end of every rhyme. Fair Warrior Maiden do tell us all, what is it that am I?"

"Not hard say I to know you well, for when ink doth dry you stand'th still. Step from your place that all might see and gaze their eyes upon letter E!"

The clans roared in laughter and cheers and Valkyrie turned to the Bard of the East to give in return her challenge,

"In ye depths of night, when all is still

I come to you unbidden, a whisper of the wills
Take many forms do I, but always shall I rise
For heat to cheeks I bring, and ample light to eyes
Some deny me, some yet try me, some call to me in secret
Yet all my power come to feel, though all not true enough to speak it!
Man of verse, without rehearse, tell what it is am I?"

A flush of pause and search of mind lit upon the Bard and in hesitation did he concede.

"Lost upon my lips the words, for my heartbeat skipped in rush. Any a poet should've know indeed that you are the embodiment of Lust!"

Cheers and laughter again rang out and Valkyrie and Bard embraced in shared appreciation.

From the South, Eilidh's champion was then chosen by Diarmuid- a towering figure armed with blunted blade. The hall fell silent as warrior Goddess Maiden and clan Giant circled round one another in measured moves.

Three great slashes followed ringing steel as Giant laid assault and Goddess Maiden did parry blows. Absorbing the fury the Valkyrie circled ever about- wearying the beastly man.

Suddenly, Morrígan caught her opponent's eye and suggestive glances ran between them. The Giant faltered in distraction and found himself there disarmed from swift and decisive exchange. Sword at his throat the crowd erupted in laughter and applause- and he knelt to receive a knight's blessing from Goddess Maiden.

From the West came a challenge of wisdom, with Diarmuid choosing from Nuala's clan a Druid shaman- offering duel in triad.

"Three keys to a fruitful life. Curious mind, compassionate heart, and courageous spirit.

To seek knowledge in all things, to extend kindness to all beings, and to face adversity with unwavering resolve - these are the paths to a life well-lived."

The clans nodded in agreement and shared in reverence, held reflection upon the shaman's verse.

The Goddess responded in time,

"Three pillars of a harmonious realm. Justice bound by mercy,

strength led by wisdom, power steadied by responsibility.
For a leader must uphold fairness while offering redemption. Wield
might with prudence. Recognize on whose account authorities are
given. Tis the way to ensure peace and prosperity ore' the lands."

"You speak of the high Goddess Maiden, and I of the low. Doth that
not make me the lesser?"

"Nay, wise Druid, for the low road arriveth first among us. Though
mine arout high, the road 'est long. Grant ye oh cup of choice to
drink from this day!"

Once more cheers erupted across the clans- the tinging of cups, the
wash of spilled ale, and the hall awaiting the next contestant.

Finally, from the North, Bevin's challenger was chosen- a Lady of Hymn
to sing of praise to Earthly mother, her voice soaring through the hall like a bird
in flight.

"I am the sonnet of the shimmering leaves, the harped plucked strings
of web in breeze. The creeping and crawling, nestled babes cooing and awe-
ing, awaiting the touch of my hand. I am the waters on the plain, the course of
torrent rains, the drink of life for all the land. I am the willow and the violet, the
rising moon at twilight, the stars glistening in the sands. I am vine ever climbing,
force of creation ever striving, I am woman, I am man."

Morrígan answering in a song of her own- spoke melody so profoundly
and intimately it seemed touch the very soul of creation.

"Spark of beauty doth shine upon ye, oh lovers of life.
Spark of conception doth ember in ye, oh husbands and wives.
Light of dear Awen be tempered in thee, oh strivers of right
Ahold of the Shadow rest still upon me, oh seeker of might
Take guard of your souls and the oaths that ye cast, oh warriors and
knights
Take care to remember the Gods and their fames, oh chaser of
sight.
Praise the Great Mother of All, that She never be forgotten
Praise the Great Father of Sky, that His all shall be allotted

Praise the Brother of the Forest, his magi in the caves
Praise the Goddess of the Waters, holy mother of trembling waves.
Feast thee now, my peoples, for soon to come are shorter days."

The challenger, moved near to tears, yielded to the Goddess Maiden's spiritual depth. Yet Morrígan drew her opposite near and walked her to hall throne to take her seat.

"Sit ye here now sister in my place, for to sing with such beauty as yours deserves highest perch this day."

Before the Lady of Hymn could refuse the offered chair, Diarmuid stepped forward and cried out for any further contenders. Smiles lit across the clans, as in a moment of mischievous inspiration the young lad himself stepped forward- Spear of Truth held hidden behind his back. Ratapskr chittered nervously about the boy's shoulder, but no heed was paid to the noble creature.

"I challenge thee, mother! Test your mettle against mine!"

Morrígan laughed, her eyes sparkling in amused affection- and she spread her arms wide in invitation of the youth to make first move.

In single, fluid motion, Diarmuid revealed deadly Spear and hurled it onwards towards his mother- certain of her invulnerability. The careening blade glinted its polished surface as firelight through the air. All gasped in collective horror as the Spear of Truth found its mark- piercing the Valkyrie's heart in terrible precision.

The Goddess Maiden staggered in shock and disbelief as she gazed upon the boy and then upon the shaft protruding from her breast. Crumpling to the ground, the skeletal tree of her youth flashed before her- she beheld Brigid in flames and once more felt Beh's torrents of scalding rage. She reached outwards towards the boy, but it was brave Fionn, First Man, who caught her hand.

With the last of her lifeforce, Morrígan saw in her lover's eyes formenting wrath- and recalled she the feel of fright. For knew she well the sufferings untold should the temperance of man be released.

"Nay my warrior husband, stay your hand...wreck not harm upon youthful folly..."

In those final words unheard, muted by blinding fury, the Goddess Maiden's journey as Protectress of Realm was ended.

The Wrath of Man

Lifeless Morrígan lay dead upon cold stone floor as deafening silence fell across the gathered clans.

First Man Fionn stood frozen- hand still outstretched from catching his fallen lover. A primal fury arose within him at the sight of his murderous son. Rage as old as time itself consumed his reason.

In hurried flash, Fionn drew hunting knife from sheath and lunged at his once-beloved son. Slicing blade finding its mark upon the boy's cheek- leaving a deep, jagged wound.

Diarmuid stumbled from the attack, hand instinctively reaching for his face- eyes rolling with anger and pain. Around the boy, clans erupted into madness. Some clamoring to defend the child in honor of the fallen Goddess, others rallying behind Fionn in grief and hellish want of revenge.

Chaotic combat ensued and father again closed to lay hands upon son. Fionn raised knife once more, readying to strike a fatal blow- and it was then that the world crafted and stewarded by Morrígan, Goddess Maiden and Valkyrie Prime, shattered as crystal against stone. Curtains of time and space spun out into a twisted storm of mortal lifetimes flinging all the lives collected across the scattered shards.

Diarmuid found himself ripped from the moment, crashing through an endless maelstrom of lives lived and lost. Each existence fleeting and burdened with an inexplicable yearning- a terrible striving for a thing never quite grasped.

The cruelty around him mirroring an inner turmoil in every lifetime. Empires rose and fell, sacred groves desecrated by clamoring armies, once-fair people subjected to unspeakable atrocities. Diarmuid himself enduring countless, unremembered incarnations - as slave, robber, murderer, and slaughtered. Endlessly witnessed he the relentless march of wanton kingdoms. Banners stained with the blood of the innocent, the constant hunger of dominion ever insatiable. Endlessly witnessed futility.

One life found Diarmuid as conqueror aboard a ship of such men, sails set for a new world- a land of savages ripe for subjugation. Charged as expedition's leader, Diarmuid the Cruel was tasked with delivering declaration and demonstration to the natives of their new masters' arrival.

With fearsome weapons, impenetrable armor, and ruthless efficiency, Diarmuid and his men descended upon unsuspecting village after village- blades and firearms sowing terror and destruction in their wake.

The air thick with stench of blood and gun smoke, screams of the dying mingling with triumphant shouts of invaders. Marched on did they through the new land, peoples bound and chained as trains of slaves. Wagoned carts of pillaged gold and silver dragged behind.

The war-scarred face of Diarmuid the Cruel rode ever ahead, calling out to those fleeing before him,

"Bring forth your leaders that they may bear witness to power true and yield the secrets of this place unto me. Only then shall the bloodletting cease."

Held out for freedom for a full campaign of such horror did they. Finally in throws of near total genocide, natives conceded themselves to terror and offered to monsters of men their chieftain's abode.

Broken bodies and burnt relics left in fields as the warband took bounties of person and prize back to waiting ships. Diarmuid, knowing now location to the voice of the land's resistance- made known to rank and slave alike that he would pay visit to chieftain in flesh alone. Only one should return with lifeblood still in their veins.

The Dagda's Bargain

Diarmuid, grim conqueror, stood before hallowed temple steps- heart pounding in anticipation of their climb. True in vow to confront the chieftain alone, walked he onward to claim the land's riches in direct decree to deposed ruler.

Ascending worn stone stairs, a lambent light of a central fire cast inviting shadows upon the walls. Following the warm glow, Diarmuid entered a sacred space- his eyes falling upon a figure seated before the flames. A man, red as a ruby scorched in hellfire.

"What seek you, bastard child of the waters?" His voice called.

"Knowledge of gold and tribute, fealty to might, your lands, your people, your harvests, your homes. Is there yet more to be sought here in these savage realms?"

The red man scoffed, *"Have you not yet subjugated enough? What more can earthly treasures offer one so steeped in blood as yours?"*

The eloquence of the chief's words piqued Diarmuid's curiosity- as the bite of gnawing hunger knowth its own.

"Who art thou?"

"I am the Dagda," replied singed lips, voice lifted in indignation. *"Once Father to noble existence, before your putrid kind. Before weapons and vicious warfare. Survived from the flames that consumed my beloved bride. Now forced to bear witness to ignorant slaughter. I ask again, Diarmuid the Cruel, what seek you?"*

"An audience with the Gods," answered conqueror.

"The gods are all dead. Your foolish mother saw to that." Baring crimson scarred chest, Dagda smiled at the agitation his words sipped upon armored warrior.

"Speak not of my mother, lest I wear your skin as belt and glove."

"Then speak that which you seek conqueror."

"I seek to be honored as God."

"There." The Dagda smiled again. *"There is truth at last from your kind. Do you recall the spear once you held, lifetimes ago? The precision of its aim, the pain it capable of inflicting?"*

Flickering memories stirred within Diarmuid – of loss, of loss of a weapon with immense power, vanished across the ages. *"I remember,"* he whispered, *"but it is lost to me now."*

"There are four such treasures in sum, indestructible are they. Even against hellspawn wolf," spoke Dagda, *"each imbued power to shape worlds, give one life eternal, foretell the spinning threads of time. Possess them together and thou a God shall be."*

"And why not claim such treasures yourself?" asked Diarmuid in suspicion of devilish forefather.

"I cannot," replied the Dagda with voice tinged in regret. *"For Brigid and I forged them for the children of Danu. They will not serve me. And when tried I gather them all to furnish protégé, stole away were they. Yet one dared not flee, that of oracle- and to you, Diarmuid, I grant power oer' that which did remain. The Stone of Destiny. It shall give aid in your search for the others."*

Red finger pointed to a primal black stone, seemingly cut from the heart of the universe itself.

"Find the treasures, possess them, and hide them well. For each life you awake anew must you continue the search. Yet be warned, in each incarnate' only in taking a human life will recall ye holy purpose and treasures claim. Fail in so doing and the existence simply passes. Pass too many such and all will be forgotten. The quest must burn your every essence when recalled so to light

through time."

Diarmuid took in the line of lives ahead of him as Dagda moved his seared red body before him. *"Kneel, that I might pass to you the secret song of the stone."*

The warlord knelt ever so hesitantly before corrupted maker, and Dagda whispered him the song of the stone.

Verse ended, empowered conqueror rose- red hand meeting his uprightness in request.

"I ask you oh slayer of murderous Valkyrie. Take blade to neck and my mortal purgatory end, Keep you mine skull as prophecy and advisor in darkest hour. Grant this or never shall you leave this place."

Without hesitation, Diarmuid drew blade- in one swift motion, the severed head of Dagda fell from rubied body. Eyes alight with the promise of godhood, Diarmuid stared upon the Stone of Destiny.

Journey to the Four Directions

Icy winds howled across snow-beaten landscapes- a relentless symphony of winter's fury. Fionn, lone traveler, trudged through knee-deep drifts, cape billowing behind him as tattered flag. It was the North sought he. A journey that had taken him across frozen tundra and forests of frost-laden pines. Bleak, bitter cold seeped to his very bones.

Approaching at last the edge of a vast, icy sea, Fionn spotted solitary figure standing beside a small boat. The man wore a wide-brimmed hat and patch covering one eye. His weathered face etched with the lines of many worlds known. The once First Man seemed to recognize him as Harbard, mysterious boatman from tales of old.

"Why travel north in conditions unyielding as these?" Harbard's voice carried over the wind like the creak of timber.

Fionn met the boatman's gaze, heart heavy with the weight of quest.

"I seek the forgiveness of my daughters," words swirling about the snow.

"And of what wrongs are ye so obliged?"

"Many," replied once First Man.

Harbard nodded knowingly. *"Aye. Forgiveness is hard won. But tis' not a gift bestowed by others. Tis' a grace rather, and it riseth from within."*

"In anger I scattered my children to the winds," confessed he to Harbard, *"surely they blame me for this suffering befallen us."*

The boatman's gloved hand fell upon Fionn's shoulder with grip firm and reassuring. *"There are three tasks hardest for any man to master. Conquering appetites, secrets keeping, and thyself knowing. Only in these trials lies true redemption, all else but only words."*

The wisdom of the seafarer rung true in Fionn's souls, *"Speak ye shrewd boatman, and yet, tis only in the eyes of my children that know I how measure mine own worth. How can I know myself apart from their judgement?"*

Harbard cast eye about the storms ahead- a brief flash of warmth struck his cheeks. Without further word, gestured he Fionn climb aboard and set sail they northward across the icy sea- wind whipping at their backs.

The white expanse of sea blended seamlessly with snow-laden sky- magnetic lights danced overhead in ribbons of green and gold til arrived they upon distant shore.

Far ahead Harbard spotted a massive white bear- standing as silent sentinel. Upon guiding boat to bank, the cloaked boatman offered a promise to once First Man.

"If not torn ye limb from limb from beast yonder, then guide you onwards shall I across compass to meet thine other three."

"Nay. *There are four yet remaining after she, for heart's center hath place as well,"* called Fionn over the winds.

"Aye, center hath place, if only yet ye survive. Go now onward to bear that I might recall noble valor."

And so Fionn did trudge up formidable ice in blizzard raging to meet the grizzled white bear awaiting.

The animal flared violence and fangs at First Man's approach. It rose onto hindlegs in offered retribution to father, and yet in intention Fionn's heart held true. In virtuous apology, prostrate he lay before the bear- and daughter Bevin did see him anew.

Awaiting uncertain end, Fionn felt the warmth of Bevin's fur fall upon his wearied head. There held they one another amid furious storm, peace slowly restoring to manly chest.

Far in the distance, the boatman smiled.

The Quests of Ages

Diarmuid and party slid past smoldering machines and gutted storefronts under sun-bleached tropic skies. Thunderous cannon mortar rained down as showers across the cityscape.

Raiding band splintered, few remained who trusted the conqueror's path. Braving great volleys of shells and flying metals, maimed Diarmuid emerged yet intact upon open square- a bubbling vat standing defiant amidst rubble. There shimmered the Cauldron of Plenty, brewing lecherous green phosphorus as if eternal stew.

"No enemies shall outlast us, with bellies ever-full and vigor ever-rising!" proclaimed he to cheers of legions restored.

As Diarmuid received chalice, so too Fionn arrived upon Eastern shores, carried forth by Harbard the mysterious. There daughter Sperling awaited, perched hawk of judgement.

"Why seek you forgiveness from I, when the cut ye bore rest upon the son?" declared Maiden of Air and Wind.

Fionn fell low, beseeching. *"Daughter, I claim not innocence nor order. Simply that mine eyes arout incomplete without thine. Beg, forgive me."*

Sperling spoke true, *"These splintered worlds are not of your doing father, it is of powers far beyond. Worry not that I held you in blame."*

And father and daughter took to wing, gliding ever-closer to that core which beckoned.

Through primal forests, grasslands vast and lifetimes apart, First Man onward did roam- seasons in rhythm. And from sunlit copse in southern realms emerged graceful doe, eyes twin mirrors of innocence lost.

"At last you meet me halfway, in lands familiar," spoke the Maiden of the Wilds, *"find you absolution in mine chase father!"*

Bound she into leafy depths, Fionn swift in pursuit.

Eons hurried, Diarmuid the Dreaded waged unending conquest. Armed with Cauldron's draught, his armies surged forth inexorable- despoiling all before them. Yet still sword eluded his grasp.

Til came the day fateful as first, invader king stood before mossy mound ancient in galactic light. There towered guardian tree Colossus, roots sprawling wide as serpentine limbs- bark hoary and dragon scaled. Nestled within knotted bole lay sword whose legend outfamed all. Sword of Destiny, forged by beloved Brigid to lend grieving smite upon wolvish plague.

Colossus bellowed warning to conqueror: *"Back, pillager of life! I, Colos-*

sus, charged Protector of Blade do repel thine covetousness. Ye may ravage worlds but this glade remains inviolate as mine own!"

Warlord gave glance again upon thirsty blade and in lustful howl clamored to wrench free stuck sword. Though famed tree did wreak havoc upon raider, Cauldron's draught ever repaired Diarmuid's body and will. Exhausted to hacked stumps, Colossus began doubt his own resolve til conqueror stormed bole to release sacred weapon.

In freeing the sword, unleashed he prodigious, hallowed sap in gout as apocalyptic amber. Colossus, as giant of green world did shudder, groaning in death throes as his many-hued leaves withered and fell- scattering upon mourning winds.

"All Father, I have failed thee." Cried he out to the heavens.

From that day forth, green became the rarest sight in any domain.

While child laid low protector of living realms, Fionn wound to western streams, where foaming breakers crashed eternal. And from those turbid depths arrowed sleek Nuala, salmon divine.

"Too long have you swum upstream father, avoiding hard consequence," admonished Maiden of Rills and Rivers. "Turn round to true repentance, facing forward to ride pure undertow."

Fionn wept then in release, salt matching salt. "You speak wisdom as sharp as any hook daughter. So long I tarried, certain in contentment. Felt pain in facing world alone, I faltered. I free myself of burden and yield to ye power oe'r my peace."

"Then have it father," came reply.

First Man then cast off raiment and dove cleanly into the deep, Nuala beside in mirthful liberation.

While cast below waters renewed errant father, above trudged fallen son, termite-gnawed Sword and Cauldron in tow.

Towards restless heart-center marched both men, where Spear did beckon.

The Age of the Goddess

At the heart of the world, where the roots of the great tree Beh once plunged deep into primordial waters- Fionn and Diarmuid stood finally again face to face. There once more upon former lands vibrant in the realm of the Goddess Maiden. Air crackled with tension, the weight of mutual quests hanging heavy between them.

Diarmuid, called upon father- knowing that one final life must be taken to claim providence. *"Where hide you the Spear, father?"*

His grip tightened upon the Sword of Destiny, blade humming with dark, insistent energy.

Fionn, seeking still absolution in this sacred center gave reply, *"Tis not spear I hide nor long for, only thine heart, oh child of mine."*

"And of these wounds you inflict upon youth, think ye able to take them back?" Diarmuid called, raising indomitable sword to strike.

Yet First Man did not move. Instead, Fionn's voice rang out in compassionate verse to prodigy,

"Stay thy hand, my son, please hear. We honor not thine mother in endless rage and fear. For such as these lead sorrow on t'wards fateful tears.

Lay down thy blade as boy again and fearful man not find. That peace shall pass t'ween us again, for in blood our peace doth bind."

Diarmuid wavered, peerless sword indecisive in his grasp. And in his moment of hesitation, dark skull's voice boomed forth, shaking the very foundations of the worlds.

The Dagda, rising as cosmic behemoth, loomed above them in planes yet unknown to form- his empty eye sockets filled with vengeance's want.

"Remember thine bargain, Diarmuid the Cruel. Of promises made, of godhood's destiny. One life yet remains to take. Silence weak forgiveness and claim ownership of realms. Spear must ye wrench from thieving clutches. Then shall we together build life anew."

Yet before Diarmuid could act in response, flash of gold light filled the chamber- Woden, shining as All Father, strode forth in rainbowed supernova.

"Enough Oh Dagda. Rise I to your call. Minions are required no longer to labor your yoke. Face you I in reprisal's challenge."

"Thief of life and treasures does reveal himself to me at last," called burnt goliath furiously to All Father, *"Defiler. Polluter of holy life. Brought ye the tortures of the hellish wolf and even destruction of thine own protectress with verminous rodent."*

For in knowing the plans of Dagda, it was All Father who sent spear and squirrel to fair maiden's realm.

"My penance is long paid for scars to Brigid. Treasures took I from you to stave off thine destructive wrath. Yet I see now this moment fated. Your path still unredeemed."

The Dagda laughed, a sound like shattering dreams, and unleashed he a wave of psychic might that brought Woden to kneel. The All Father struggling against the onslaught bent, divine essence flickering like candle tossed in tempest.

"Your thieving guardians have fallen before mine champion boy. Now left only to call forth spear will this plague of existence be ended."

In that moment of darkest despair, death faced down upon luminous sky god ominously. Yet, looking beyond the hollow sockets of cosmic ghoul Dagda, the All Father saw a flash of gold in second streak upon the lands.
From it emerged Valkyrie Morrígan- healed of her wounds.

Burst forth she from central sky as beacon of hope and light returned-Spear of Truth astride in her grasp. Once rodent emissary of Ceridwen too strode mightily in perch upon her shoulder in splendid arms. Flawlessly floated she in challenge to rubied forefather- Ratatpskr chittering excitedly.

> **"Great Grandfather.**
> **Thine grief runs deep, yet reign of pain must end.**
> **For love of right and noble life doth spear of true defend.**
> **From Fate's own hand, to mine 'twas sent,**
> **That shall forth bring I an end to thine descent.**
> **Mark ever true, yet in mercy stab yields to me**
> **Slip of tip before skin can it find, cut yields to me**
> **Thrust of force born in mind, yet it yields to me**
> **Yield so to me same Great Grandfather, 'fore your power is recalled**
> **as villainy."**

"Murderous Valkyrie thine arout not capable of my conquest," Ghoulish Dagda called.

Morrígan charged ever forward, Spear of Truth blazing with the fury of the atom's power. Met she the Dagda in clash of cosmic proportions, their battle shaking reality itself. Yet she was no match for rubied warrior.

As titans struggled, Fionn and Diarmuid looked to one other. A moment of insight genuine and pure passed before their eyes to one another. In a glance, forgiveness sought and granted- and as one, both turned their hearts and minds to prayerful thanks and surrender to the Goddess herself.

Upon finally hearing in unity's cry the voices of those destined to worship her, the Goddess Ceridwen appeared once more. Now second to none. Now, Goddess of All. She who is of the Shadows. Nurturer of Great Beh. Step-Mother to Stag, Raven and Wolf. Birth Mother to Angels. Weaver of time. Mistress of Form. Bright, Heavenly Ceridwen now Protectress of Realm. The Age of the Goddess arrived.

Her presence a staggering moonlight banishing abhorrence and healing wounds sown of old. In seeing her return, Dagda, suspended his battle against Valkyrie Morrígan and All Father.

"Praise dear Goddess Ceridwen, I welcome thee at last as Mind." Spoke Dagda as his image retreated from manifest planes.

Fionn and Diarmuid, father and son, embraced at last again- each with quest now ended. Morrígan's daughters, husband and son returned to her. Woden onward gazing with pride and love, held fast again basking in the light of the Goddess. Knowing he that a new age had dawned, where children of the Earth would commune and envision with gods t'ward ever nobler ground.

And so, the Book of Awen concludes- savor the wisdom of ages revealed- marvel the power of human spirit divine.

BIOGRAPHIES

ANDREW BUCKNER is a noted poet, critic, author, actor, and experimental musician.

TOM SNARSKY is the author of the chapbooks *Threshold* (Another New Calligraphy) and *Complete Sentences* (Broken Sleep Books), as well as the full-length collections *Light-Up Swan* and *Reclaimed Water* (both from Ornithopter Press). His book *A Letter From The Mountain & Other Poems* is forthcoming in 2025 from Animal Heart Press. He lives in the mountains of northwestern Virginia with his wife Kristi and their cats. You can find him on Twitter, Instagram, and Bluesky @tomsnarsky

BERNARD PEARSON's work appears in over one hundred publications worldwide including *Aesthetica Magazine, The Edinburgh Review,* and *The York Literary Review.* In 2017, a selection of his poetry *In Free Fall* was published by Leaf Press. In 2019, he won second prize in The Aurora Prize for Writing for his poem Manor Farm.

ALEX RUSSELL is a writer and designer based out of Northern Virginia. He loves visiting art museums, collecting physical media, and spending time with his cat. Originally from Ukraine, he dreams of an early retirement in Mexico City. He is on Tumblr @wernerherzogshave

JESSE DOMINGUEZ is an underpaid 30-something in the North-Central United States of America. The poetry he writes is inspired by wide-open highways, conversations with passerbys, past mistakes, and the first snow of the season. Jesse is always prepared for a shared cup of coffee and a moment of your time. You can find more of his poetry on Tumblr at @hauntedguardenking

MILENA FILIPPS is a history student in Germany. She enjoys reading works by Marcel Proust, Jane Austen and Goethe as well as learning about art history and historical architecture. Her essays *Academic Reading and My Glasses* (2023) were published by *Livina Press*, while her poems appeared in *Swim Press* (2023), *The Field Guide Poetry Magazine* (2023), *RIC Journal* (2021) and *Mosaik* (2020), among others. You can find her on Instagram @milenafilipps

BIOGRAPHIES

MARGARET MONTET's narratives of place blend memoir, research, and the arts. She's a college librarian and completed the Pan European MFA Program at Cedar Crest College specializing in Creative Nonfiction. Margaret blends these skills when teaching music history courses to older adults and public speaking to college students. Her creative nonfiction has been published in *The Bangalore Review, Pink Pangea, Library Journal, Mature Years, America in WWII, Edible Jersey,* and other fine periodicals and anthologies. Her collection of travel essays, *Nerd Traveler,* was published in July, 2021, and *Brooklyn Family Album* will be published in September 2024.

SKYE COOLEY is a professor of media and strategic communications at Oklahoma State University and the founder of the MESA group. He is a practitioner and instructor of Ba Gua Zhang through Internal Arts International, a Druidic spiritualist in the Order of Bards, Ovates, and Druids, and an avid outdoorsman. He aspires to be a sage of the forest and is known by his daughter as the Black Stag.

EDWARD MICHAEL SUPRANOWICZ is the grandson of Irish and Lithuanian/Russian/Ukrainian immigrants. He grew up on a small farm in Appalachia. He has a grad background in painting and printmaking. Some of his artwork has recently or will soon appear in *Fish Food, Streetlight, Another Chicago Magazine, Door Is A Jar, The Phoenix, and The Harvard Advocate.* Edward is also a published poet who has had over 700 poems published and been nominated for the Pushcart Prize multiple times.

MELINDA SNYDER lives with her husband and two feline kids in Spring Valley, CA. In her free time she enjoys all kinds of art: crocheting, sewing, beadwork, drawing and painting. She is inspired by the diversity and beauty of colors and textures found in nature and has enjoyed crafting things with her creativity and her own two hands since she was very young. She is also a musician although these days she spends more time listening to music than playing it. Facebook and Etsy: Cobalt Owl Creations. Instagram @cobaltowlcreations